Foreign Fruit

TREY FRY

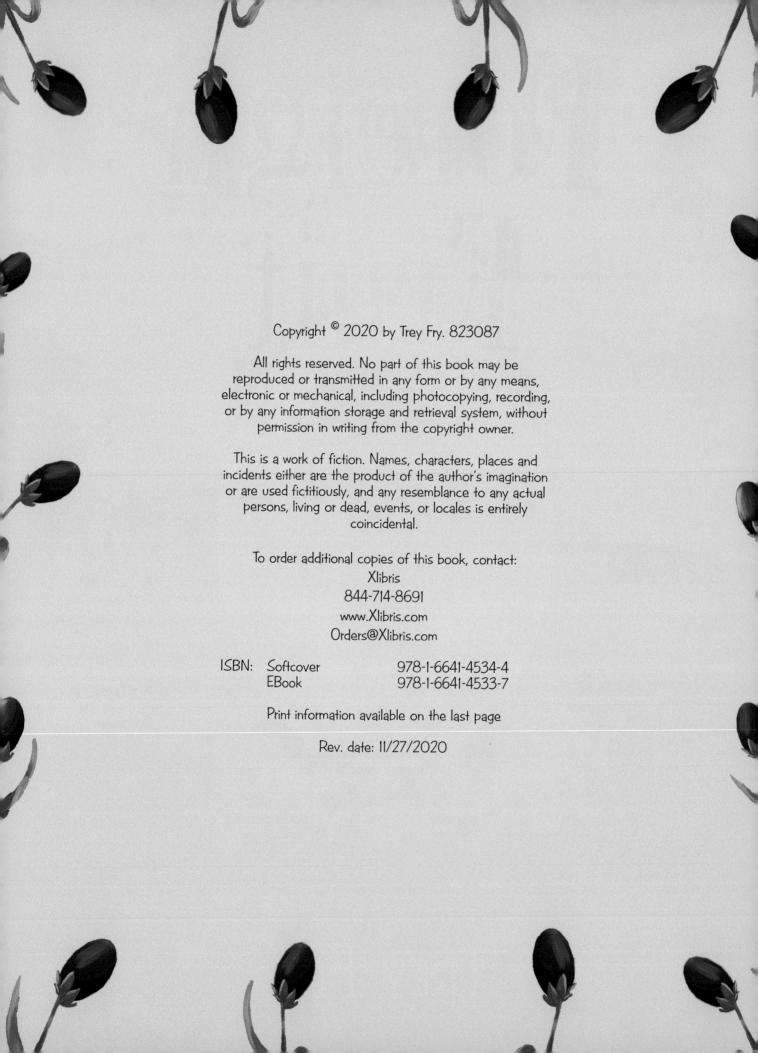

To order additional copies of this book, contact:
Xlibris
844-714-8691
www.Xlibris.com
Orders@Xlibris.com

ISBN: Softcover   978-1-6641-4534-4
        EBook   978-1-6641-4533-7

Print information available on the last page

Rev. date: 11/27/2020

Foreign Fruit

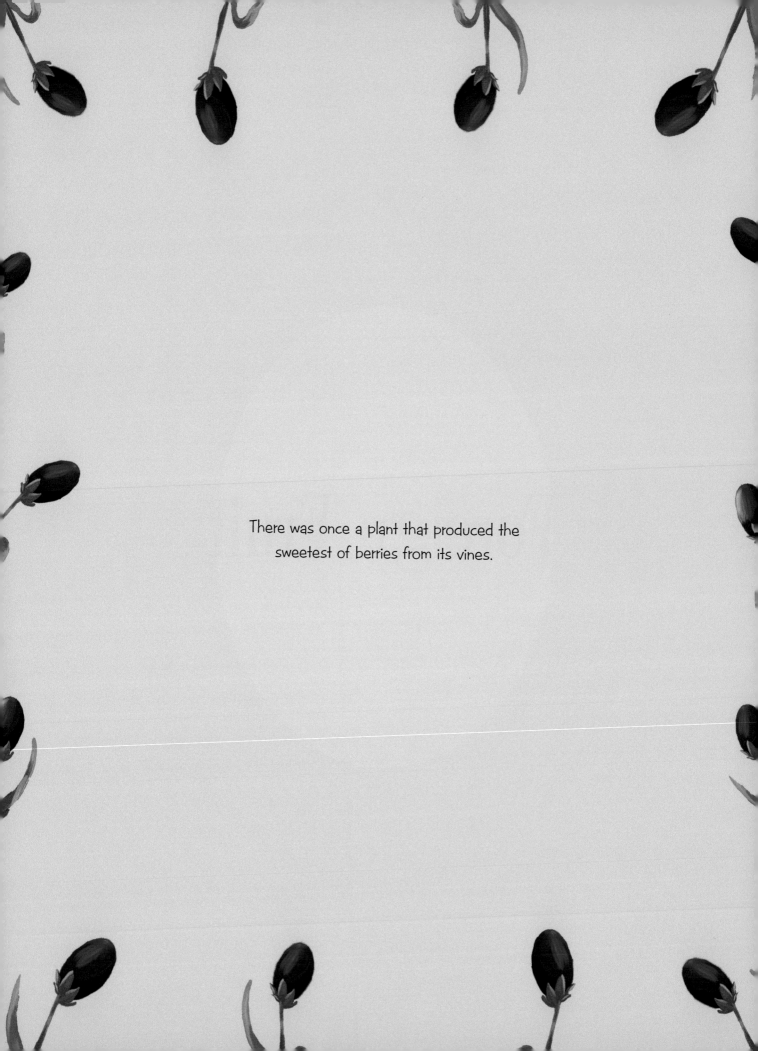

There was once a plant that produced the
sweetest of berries from its vines.

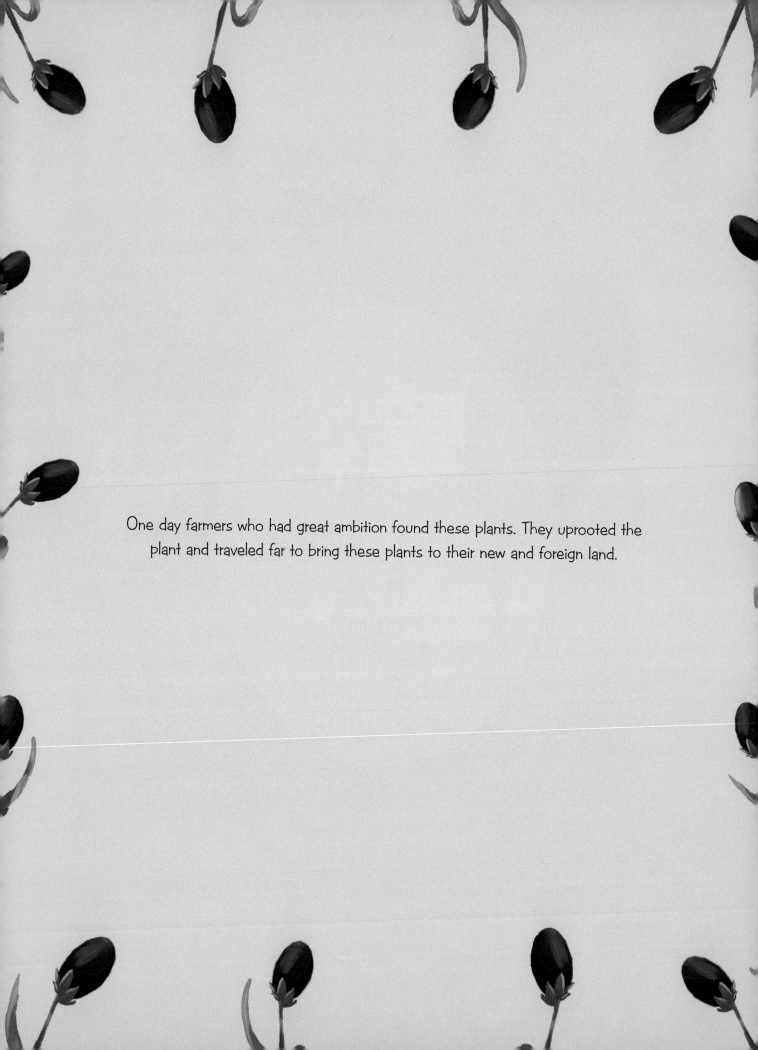

One day farmers who had great ambition found these plants. They uprooted the plant and traveled far to bring these plants to their new and foreign land.

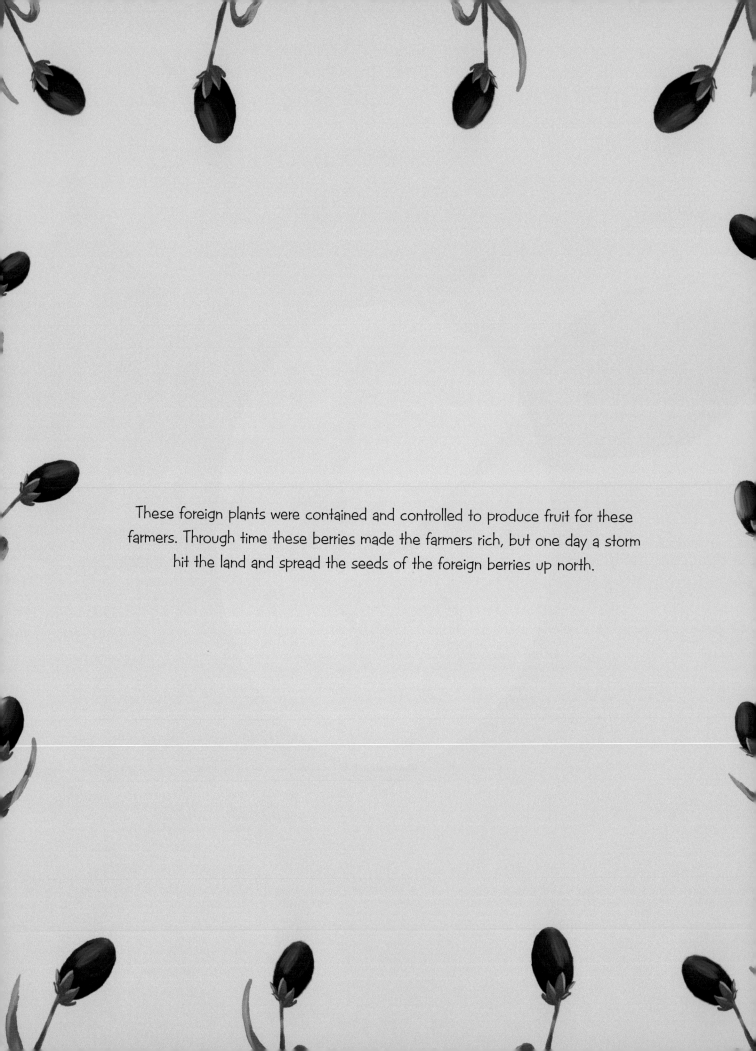

These foreign plants were contained and controlled to produce fruit for these farmers. Through time these berries made the farmers rich, but one day a storm hit the land and spread the seeds of the foreign berries up north.

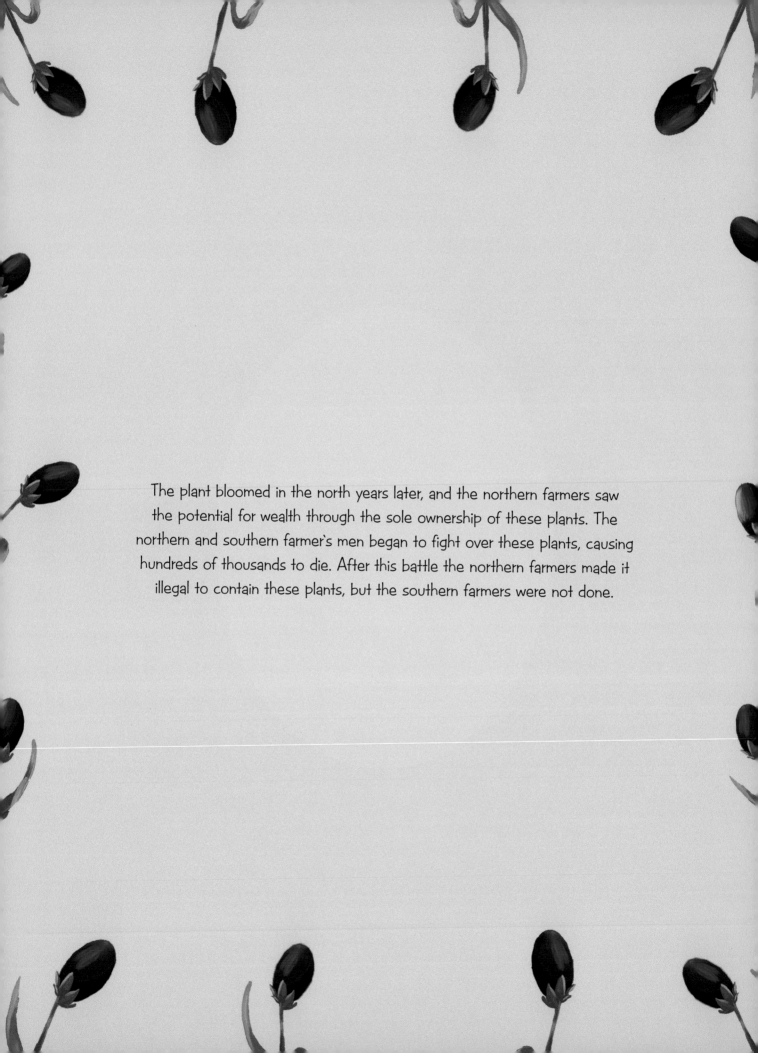

The plant bloomed in the north years later, and the northern farmers saw the potential for wealth through the sole ownership of these plants. The northern and southern farmer's men began to fight over these plants, causing hundreds of thousands to die. After this battle the northern farmers made it illegal to contain these plants, but the southern farmers were not done.

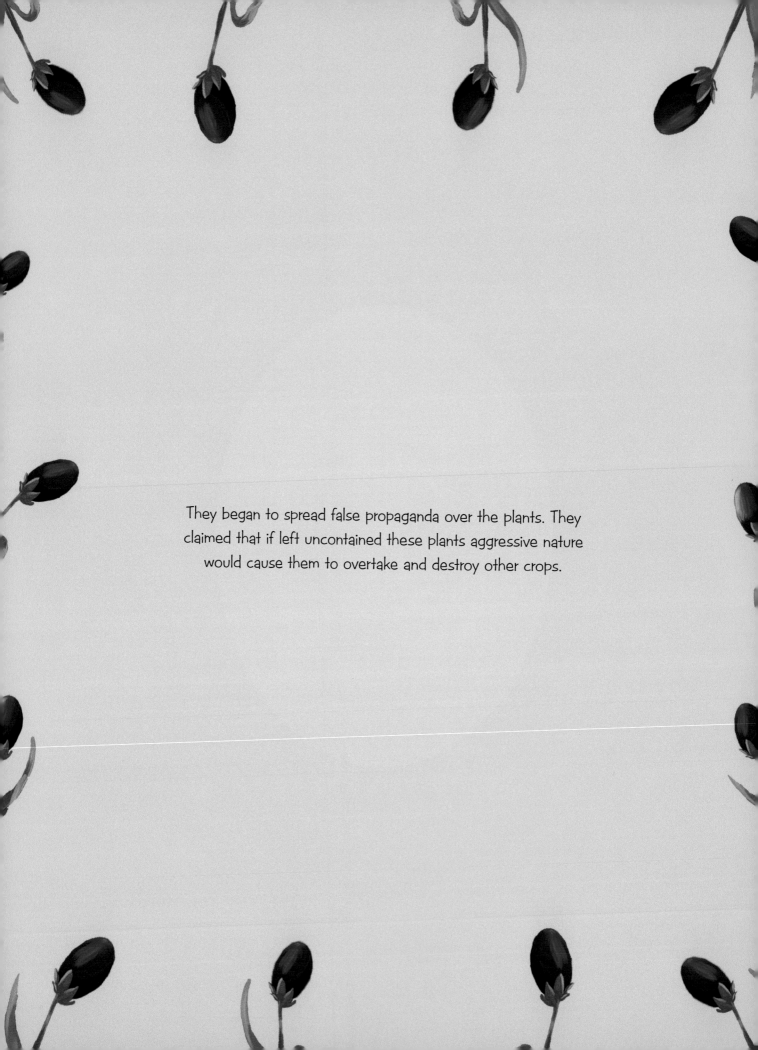

They began to spread false propaganda over the plants. They claimed that if left uncontained these plants aggressive nature would cause them to overtake and destroy other crops.

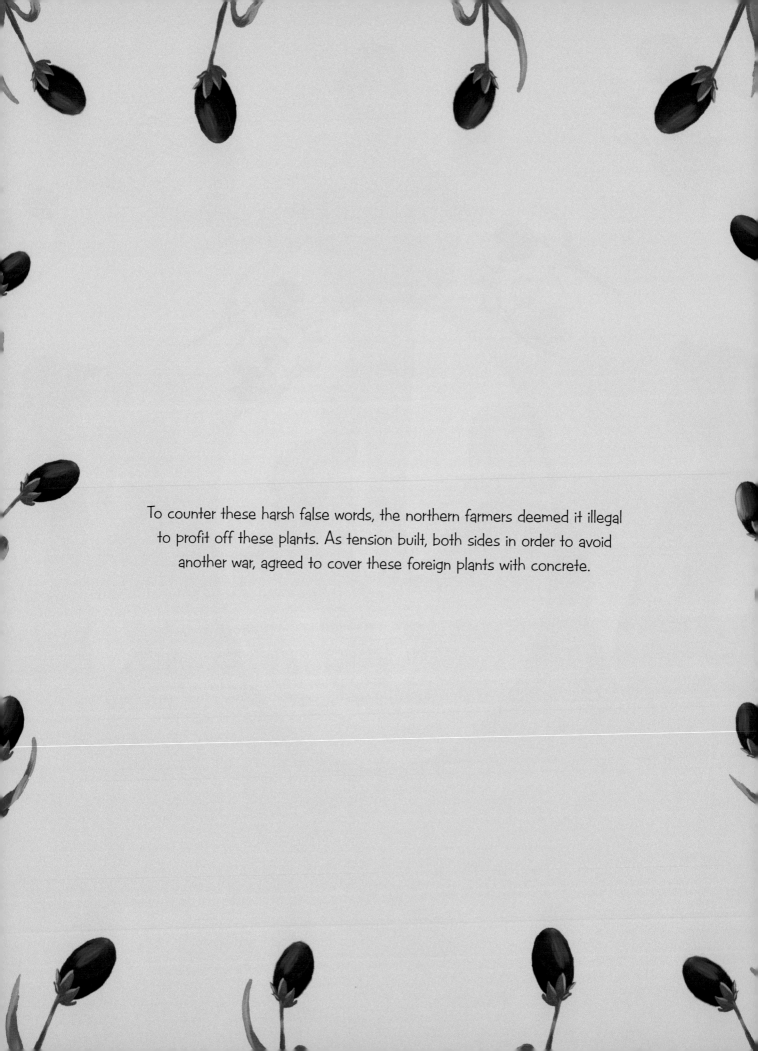

To counter these harsh false words, the northern farmers deemed it illegal to profit off these plants. As tension built, both sides in order to avoid another war, agreed to cover these foreign plants with concrete.

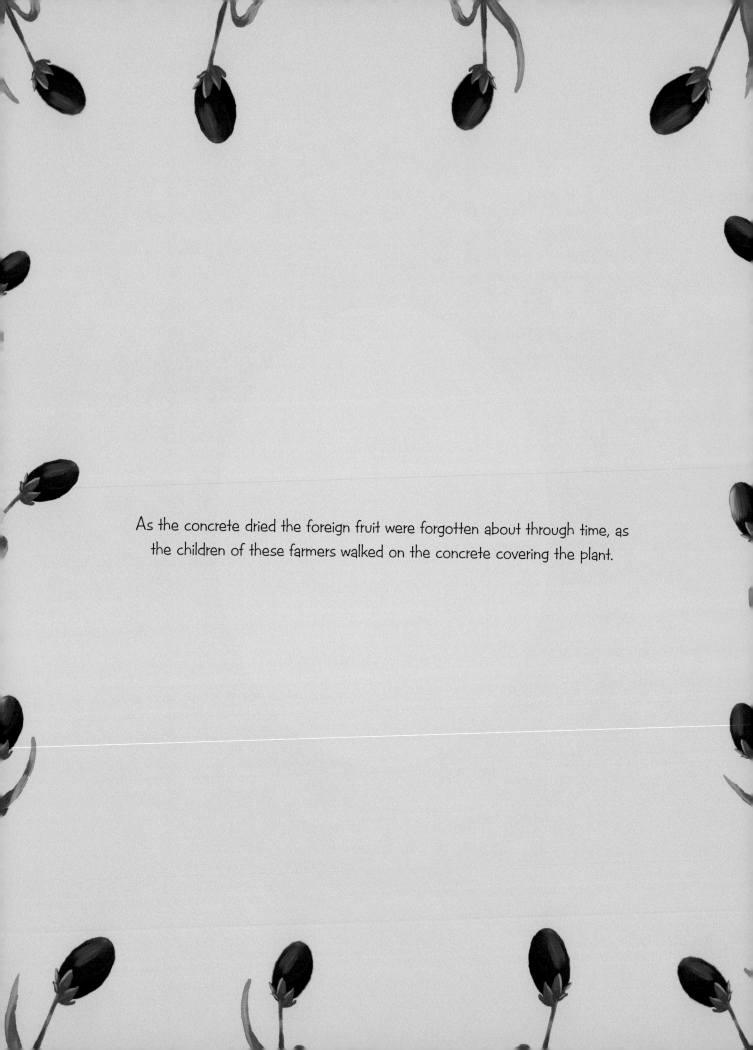

As the concrete dried the foreign fruit were forgotten about through time, as the children of these farmers walked on the concrete covering the plant.

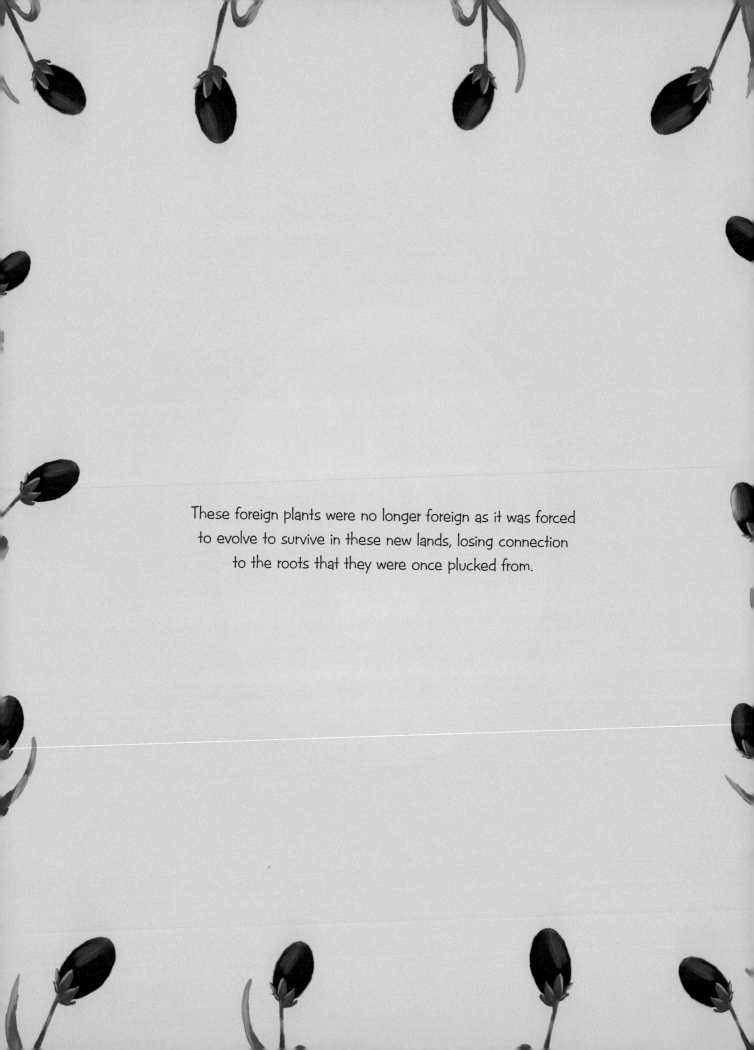

These foreign plants were no longer foreign as it was forced
to evolve to survive in these new lands, losing connection
to the roots that they were once plucked from.

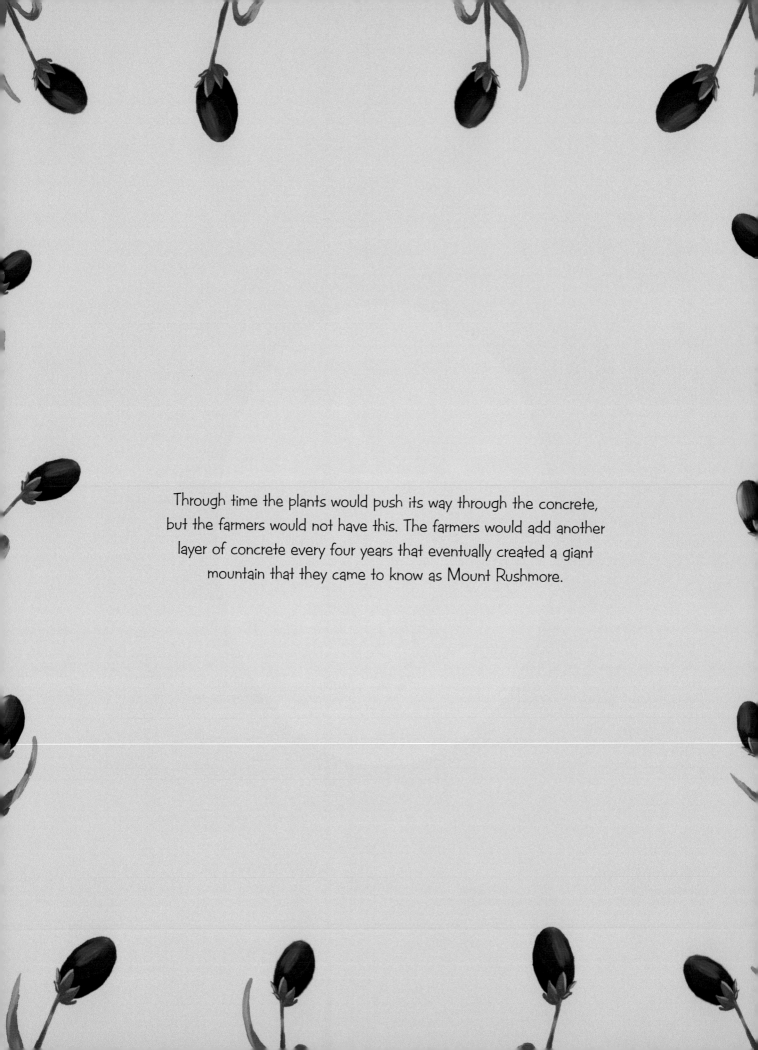

Through time the plants would push its way through the concrete, but the farmers would not have this. The farmers would add another layer of concrete every four years that eventually created a giant mountain that they came to know as Mount Rushmore.

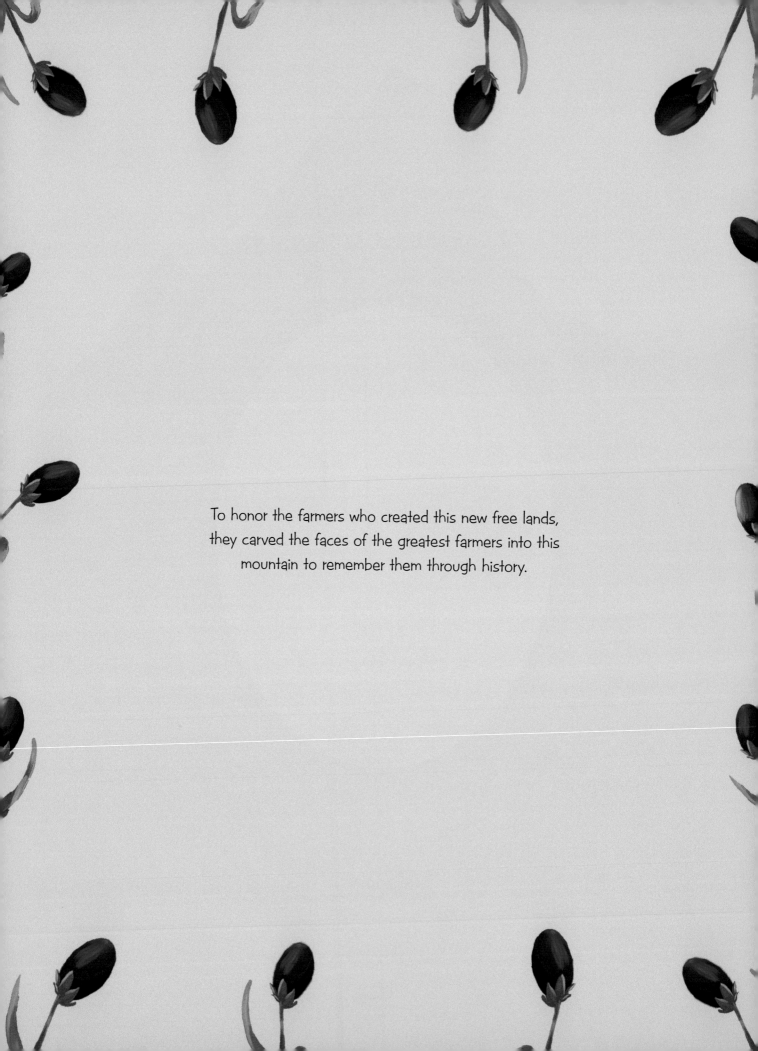

To honor the farmers who created this new free lands,
they carved the faces of the greatest farmers into this
mountain to remember them through history.

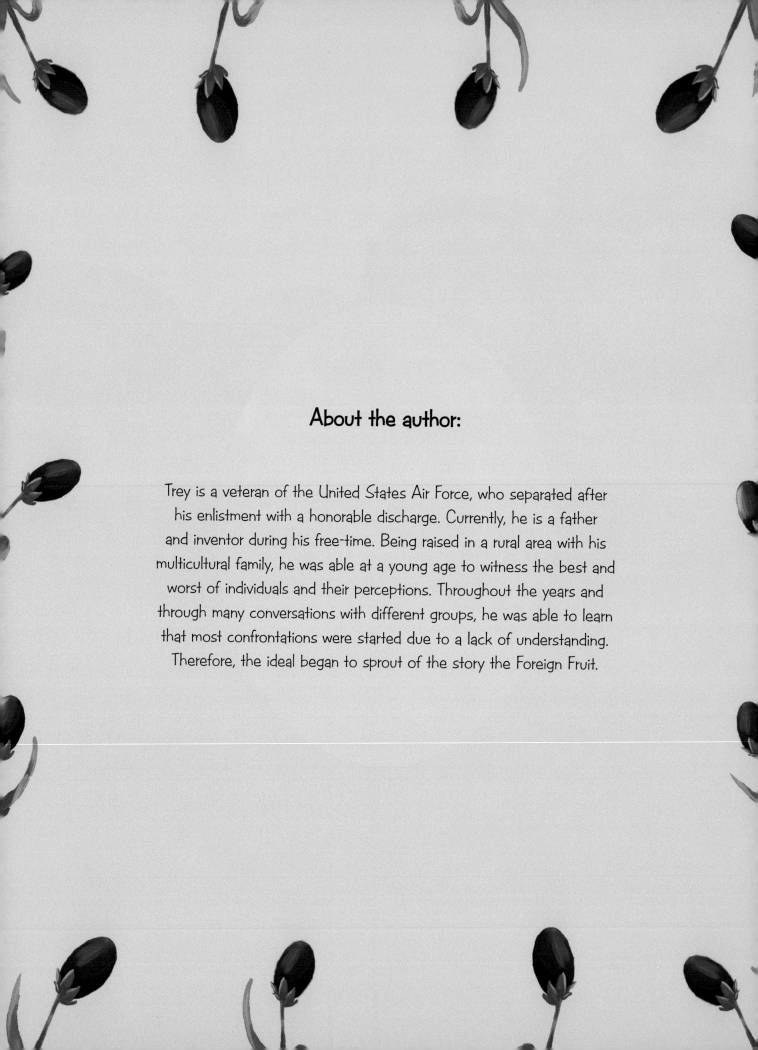

About the author:

Trey is a veteran of the United States Air Force, who separated after his enlistment with a honorable discharge. Currently, he is a father and inventor during his free-time. Being raised in a rural area with his multicultural family, he was able at a young age to witness the best and worst of individuals and their perceptions. Throughout the years and through many conversations with different groups, he was able to learn that most confrontations were started due to a lack of understanding. Therefore, the ideal began to sprout of the story the Foreign Fruit.

Printed in the United States
By Bookmasters